Hi, I'm Jessica.

I've been on work experience at

an animal charity.

Some animals are rescued from

cruel owners.

Some are sick or injured.

It's not easy to get to work with animals but I was determined! Mum helped me to write a letter to Sunny Fields. This is what we wrote.

27 Red Land
Barton
BT 19 8TD

15th March

Dear Mr Andrews,

Please can I do my work experience at
Sunny Fields?

I love animals and I am very good with them.
I have a dog, two cats, a rabbit and a hamster.

I get very good school reports.

Thank you

Jessica Roberts

It worked! Mr Andrews asked me and my mum to an interview.
Mr Andrews asked me about my sheepdog, Shep.
I told him I feed him and take him for walks twice a day.
He was pleased.

He said I'd need to have tetanus injections.
Mum signed a form.
Then he said, 'See you after the holidays! Wear old clothes!'
I was really excited.

On my first Monday Mr Andrews showed me round.

There were lots of cats and dogs.

There were lots of farm animals, too!

Mr Andrews said it was important to get the animals fit and well.

It was also important to find them good homes.

CATTERY

KENNELS

RABBITS

'You'll see things that will upset you,'
warned Mr Andrews.

He was right! I saw a dog blinded by
an airgun.

I saw a cat that had been hit by a car.

I saw three puppies. Someone had
thrown them into the canal.

It was awful.

Then Mr Andrews took me to the kennels.

'These dogs are ready for new homes,' he said. 'You'll work here.'

I met Ben, my supervisor.

Mr Andrews said I'd learn a lot from watching Ben.

Each dog has a kennel. The kennels
are great!

They have two parts. One part is a bed,
the other part is a run.

The floor is made of concrete. Concrete
is easy to clean.

The walls are made from wire mesh.

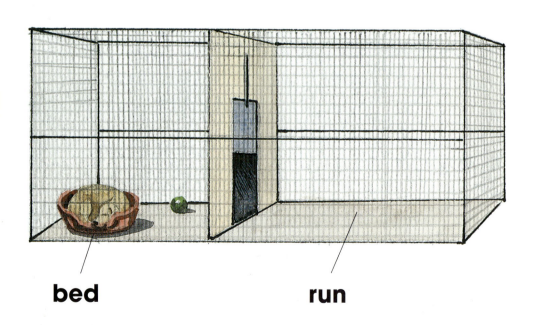

bed   **run**

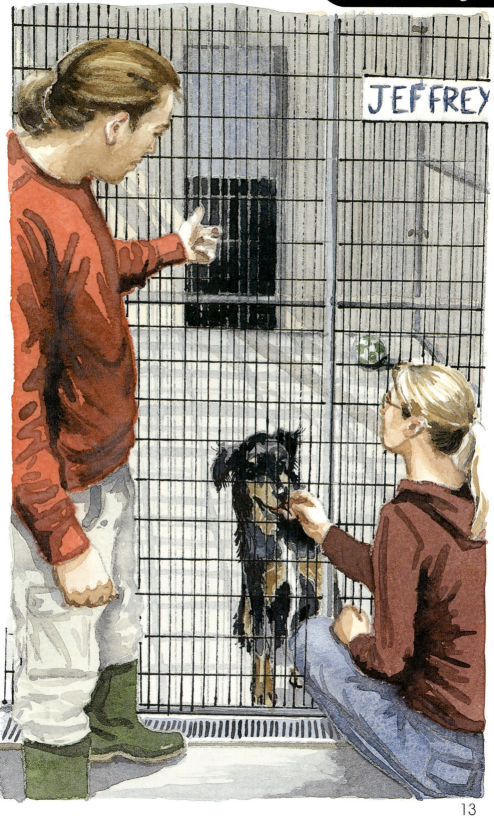

JEFFREY

Jess, you can take Bruno for a walk.

The animals are given cool names.

One dog was called Charlie Collie.

My favourite dog was Bruno Boxer.

His owner had not looked after him.

Ben was hoping to find him a new home.

I took Bruno for a walk.

I worked from 9 o'clock until 5 o'clock every day.

I got very tired.

Sometimes the weather was cold, wet and windy.

One day it was *really* windy. I put on a hat to keep me warm.

The wind whipped it off. It landed in Bruno's water bowl.

Ben and I couldn't stop laughing!

Every day there was a lot to do.
First Ben and I checked the dogs and
took them for walks.
Then we cleaned the kennels. I used
a bucket and a shovel.
I wore gloves, overalls and boots to
keep myself clean.
It was a really smelly job!
It's lucky I'm not squeamish!

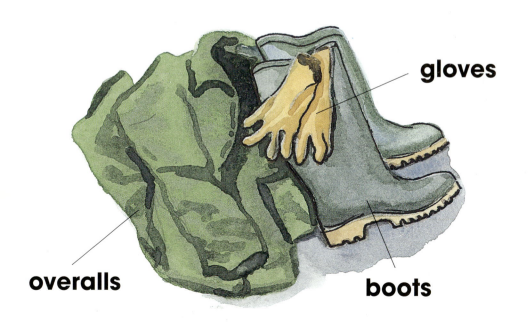

gloves

overalls

boots

One day I found Bruno lying down in his kennel.

I could see that something was wrong.

He had been sick. I told Ben.

Ben phoned the vet, and we tried to make him comfortable.

I was really upset.

The vet gave Bruno an injection to help him get well.

We moved Bruno away from the other dogs.

We didn't want them to get ill, too.

Bruno didn't get well. He died the next day.

I cried for ages.

My work experience finished today.

It's been brilliant.

Mr Andrews says I can come back at weekends. YES!

I won't be paid, but it's what I want to do.

I might think about doing a college course now.